Butterfly Wishes

Tiger Streak's Tale

Butterfly Wishes

Tiger Streak's Tale

Jennifer Castle

illustrated by Tracy Bishop

BLOOMSBURY

NEW YORK   LONDON   OXFORD   NEW DELHI   SYDNEY

First published in the United States of America in December 2017
by Bloomsbury Children's Books
www.bloomsbury.com

Bloomsbury is a registered trademark of Bloomsbury Publishing Plc

For information about permission to reproduce selections from this book, write to
Permissions, Bloomsbury Children's Books, 1385 Broadway, New York, New York 10018
Bloomsbury books may be purchased for business or promotional use. For information on
bulk purchases please contact Macmillan Corporate and Premium Sales Department at
specialmarkets@macmillan.com

Library of Congress Cataloging-in-Publication Data
Names: Castle, Jennifer, author.
Title: Tiger Streak's tale / by Jennifer Castle.
Description: New York : Bloomsbury, 2017. | Series: Butterfly wishes ; 2
Summary: Sisters Addie and Clara are called upon by the Wishing Wings to help a
newly emerged butterfly, Tiger Streak, who was cursed to think she is a bee.
Identifiers: LCCN 2017007281
ISBN 978-1-68119-373-1 (paperback) • ISBN 978-1-68119-492-9 (hardcover)
ISBN 978-1-68119-374-8 (e-book)
Subjects: | CYAC: Butterflies—Fiction. | Bees—Fiction. | Wishes—Fiction. |
Magic—Fiction. | Sisters—Fiction.
Classification: LCC PZ7.C268732 Tig 017 | DDC [Fic]—dc23
LC record available at https://lccn.loc.gov/2017007281

Typeset by Westchester Publishing Services
Printed and bound in the U.S.A. by Berryville Graphics Inc., Berryville, Virginia
2 4 6 8 10 9 7 5 3 1 (paperback)
2 4 6 8 10 9 7 5 3 1 (hardcover)

All papers used by Bloomsbury Publishing, Inc., are natural, recyclable products
made from wood grown in well-managed forests. The manufacturing processes
conform to the environmental regulations of the country of origin.

For S. and C.,
the butterfly spirits in my life

Butterfly Wishes

Tiger Streak's Tale

PROLOGUE

An early morning breeze whistled through the woods, making the leaves of a huge willow tree shimmy and shake. Two butterflies sat perched on the edge of a deep hollow in the tree's trunk, and the breeze made their colorful wings ripple.

The butterflies barely noticed. They were busy staring into the hollow, where they saw three small gray shapes hanging down. Each one was a chrysalis, and inside were caterpillars waiting to emerge as something beautiful and new.

One of the butterflies, Sky Dance, had pink and turquoise wings splattered with cloud patterns. She pointed one of her antennae to a fourth shape: the crumpled remains of a chrysalis that had already opened.

"Just yesterday, you were right in there," she whispered to the other butterfly, Shimmer Leaf.

"Whoa," muttered Shimmer Leaf, stretching her wings out flat. They were bright purple, peach, and mint green with leaf patterns. "Wishing Wing chrysalides should be glowing and gold . . . but these just look wrong."

"We suspect there's a dark enchantment on them," said Sky Dance. "When you emerged, you didn't know who you were, or even that you were a Wishing Wing!"

"I was so scared . . ." said Shimmer Leaf, shuddering at the memory.

"The worst part was that you didn't know you had to earn your magic by granting a wish to a human child before sunset. You almost lost your magic forever, and all Wishing Wing magic would have been weakened!" Sky Dance paused, staring sadly into the hollow. "I'm worried that these chrysalides will have the same problem."

"Who would cast a dark enchantment like this?" asked Shimmer Leaf. "Who would want to make Wishing Wing magic disappear?"

"We don't know, but hopefully we'll find out soon."

Suddenly, one of the gray chrysalides began to move, wiggling and jiggling. It wasn't because of the breeze.

This chrysalis was getting ready to burst.

"I'm nervous," Shimmer Leaf said softly, touching one of her wings to one of Sky Dance's wings.

"Me too," replied Sky Dance. "But we have to be strong and brave. If our friend is under enchantment, she'll need our help."

"And we'll have to find it on the far side of the meadow," added Shimmer Leaf.

The sisters exchanged a glance. They both knew what that meant.

They turned back to the chrysalis just as it began to open . . .

CHAPTER ONE

Addie Gibson opened her eyes.
A stream of golden morning sunlight peeked past her window curtains. She sat up in bed and looked around. For a moment, everything felt the same as it had the day before.

Her room was still filled with unpacked boxes, since her family had just moved to a new house. The walls were bare with that half-gross, half-sweet smell of fresh turquoise paint. Her best friend, Violet, was still far away, back in the city where Addie used to live, and her new neighborhood, Brook Forest, was still surrounded by way too much nature.

Then she remembered:

Butterflies! Wishes!

MAGIC!

Yesterday had been the day Addie discovered it all.

Deep in the woods behind her house, there was a secret grove filled with enchanted butterflies called Wishing Wings. They could talk, grant wishes, and work extraordinary magic. The Wishing Wings needed Addie and her younger sister, Clara, to help newly hatched butterflies earn their magic by making a wish come true for a human child. Someone, or some*thing*, had cast a dark enchantment on these "New Blooms." If Addie and Clara didn't succeed in their task, the New Blooms would lose their powers forever and weaken the magic of all the Wishing Wings.

Addie shuddered at the thought as she touched the gold bracelet on her wrist. It kept her close to Violet—that had been the wish her new friend, the Wishing Wing princess Sky Dance, granted her. Sky Dance believed another New Bloom would emerge today who might need help granting its first wish. Addie and Sky Dance could share thoughts if they were near each other, so Addie listened hard inside her head.

But she heard only silence, until . . .

"Stop! Stop it now!"

It was Clara shouting from across the

hallway. Addie burst out of bed and into Clara's room.

Clara was huddled in a corner, cradling a little ball of orange fur to her chest: her new kitten, Squish. Clara had helped Shimmer Leaf, Sky Dance's sister and the first of the newly hatched Wishing Wings, break her enchantment by catching the butterfly and then setting her free. In return, Shimmer Leaf granted Clara's wish for a real live pet of her own . . . and now Clara's stuffed kitten was a real one.

The magic of it had been amazing, but not as amazing as seeing Clara snap out of her sadness about moving to Brook Forest.

Even Addie's parents were happy about Squish joining the family—they thought he was a stray kitten the girls found in the backyard. Only Addie's dog, Pepper, wasn't a fan of their new feline friend. Right now he was running back and forth in front of Clara, barking at Squish.

"Pepper!" snapped Addie, grabbing his collar. "Bad boy!"

She picked him up and put him out of the room, then closed the door.

"I'm sorry, Clara," she said, kneeling on the floor next to her sister. "Sorry to you, too, Squish. Pepper has to get used to the fact that he's no longer the only cute one in the house!"

Addie reached out to pet Squish. He instantly started purring and stretched out on the floor. She rubbed his soft orange-and-white-striped belly.

"Can you believe it?" asked Clara. "I woke up and thought maybe it was all just a dream, but then I felt this fuzzy warm thing curled up next to me."

"I know," said Addie. "It seems unreal to me, too. But it *was* real, wasn't it?"

Clara nodded, smiling, then stood up and went to her window. It looked out on their backyard and the woods beyond. Addie joined her.

"What do you think Sky Dance and Shimmer Leaf are doing right now?" asked Clara. "When do you think we'll see them again?"

"I don't know," replied Addie. "But I have a feeling it'll be soon."

Clara slid open her window and rested her forehead against the screen, breathing in the fresh morning air. "I think I could get used to living in the country."

Suddenly, voices came drifting through the open window. They were kid voices, but not happy ones. Someone was yelling at someone else. They sounded pretty mad.

Clara shot Addie a curious look.

"I'll go investigate," said Addie.

"You mean, *eavesdrop*?" teased Clara.

"Hey, stop picking up big words from Mom and Dad. I can be curious, can't I?"

Addie got dressed with lightning speed. She rushed downstairs and out the back door.

"I can't believe you!" shouted a boy's voice. "You ruined it!"

"I didn't mean to!" came a girl's voice, just as loud and angry.

Addie heard a loud *thump*. She watched as a soccer ball came crashing through the bushes that separated her yard from the one next door.

"That's what I think of your art project!" yelled the boy.

The ball rolled to a stop right in front of the deck. Addie picked it up and stood there for a few moments. She looked up at Clara's window, where Clara had been watching with Squish in her arms. Clara shrugged, then disappeared.

"Hi," came a voice.

Addie turned to see a girl standing at the bushes. She seemed about the same age as Addie, with long red hair in a braid. She wore a T-shirt with the collar cut off, and two different kinds of sneakers. *Well,* thought Addie, *at least her socks match.*

"Hi," Addie said, and held up the ball. "Is this yours?"

Now Addie could see that the ball had been painted all white, with a goofy face on it. The face had wide eyes, a big nose, and a crooked smile. It even had earrings and a patch of curly red hair.

Addie couldn't help it—she let out a laugh.

"This is a really good face!" she said.

"Thanks," said the girl, but she looked embarrassed about it.

"I'm Addie. We just moved in a few days ago."

"I'm Morgan."

They were quiet as Morgan approached and took the ball. It was awkward, meeting new people. Even ones who live right next door.

The bushes rustled, and now a woman appeared on the edge of the yard.

"Hey, Mom," called Morgan when she saw the woman. "This is Addie, our new neighbor. Addie, this is my mom."

Morgan's mom smiled and waved. "Otherwise known as Mrs. Werner. I was planning to bring over some cookies tomorrow, so we could all meet properly. But I see that, once again, Morgan has gone and done things her own way."

She gave Morgan a stern look.

"Calvin kicked the ball over here!" said Morgan. "I was just getting it back."

"Oh," said Mrs. Werner, but her expression grew even more stern. "Yes, he told me you destroyed his new soccer ball."

"I thought it was an old one he doesn't use anymore!" Morgan added.

Mrs. Werner shook her head. "Honey, you can't keep painting things that aren't supposed to be painted. I bought you paper and blank canvases. Paint those!"

"But . . ." protested Morgan.

"Addie, it was nice meeting you," said Mrs. Werner. "Tell your parents I'm looking forward to meeting them too."

Mrs. Werner went back to her yard.

Morgan sighed. She looked at the ball again and then at Addie. "But I don't want to paint on paper or canvas," she said softly. "I just like taking real things and making them look different. Mom doesn't understand. She calls me The Troublemaker."

Addie smiled back. "That's a good one. My mom calls me Little Miss Overthink."

Morgan and Addie laughed together. The awkwardness was gone, and Addie felt more comfortable now. *Hey!* she thought. *We might like each other!*

Would Morgan be her first new friend in Brook Forest? *Human* friend, that is?

A moment later, Addie heard and felt something flutter past her ear. She looked up to see a flash of color in the air above.

Make that two flashes of color.

It was Sky Dance and Shimmer Leaf!

As soon as Addie realized this, she felt Sky Dance's thoughts in her head. *Quick! Get Clara! Meet us in the woods!*

This could mean only one thing: another New Bloom had emerged, and the Wishing Wings needed help!

"I'm so sorry," said Addie to Morgan as she started backing away. "There's kind of an emergency. I've got to find my sister right now."

Morgan looked confused. "An emergency?"

"I can't explain it. I just have to go."

Now Morgan looked deeply hurt. She dropped her head and turned toward the bushes, her shoulders sagging.

Addie watched Morgan walk away, imagining Morgan's point of view. To her, it must have looked like Addie had suddenly, randomly, changed her mind about talking to Morgan. But that was totally not the case!

Addie wasn't sure what else to say, so she didn't say anything.

She just ran into the house, feeling absolutely awful. She vowed to herself to make it up to Morgan somehow. But right now, Sky Dance and Shimmer Leaf were depending on her.

CHAPTER TWO

C lara!" shouted Addie to her sister's window. "Come quick! The butter-flies need us!"

But Clara was already stepping out the back door. Addie jumped, startled.

"I know," said Clara. "I got the same message from Shimmer."

"We should tell Mom that we're going for a walk."

"Already done."

Addie was impressed. "Nice work."

"I think of things, too, you know," said Clara, but she didn't sound mad. Just proud of herself.

Addie reached out and took her sister's hand. Together, they walked past the row of evenly spaced trees at the back edge of their yard and into the thick, green world of the woods.

Addie was surprised to find she already recognized certain trees and rocks. It really was becoming *their* woods now, after just a day! She couldn't help but smile, remembering how scared she'd been of all this twenty-four hours ago.

Eventually, the girls reached Silk Meadow, a sun-drenched clearing of tall grass that marked the entrance to

Wishing Wing Grove. Addie felt something land on her arm. A familiar tickle.

"Hi, Sky Dance," she said, raising her arm so she was eye level with her butterfly friend. "Long time no see."

Sky Dance flapped her wings. They were just as big and beautiful as Addie remembered. Sky Dance tilted her furry pink head as if she were thinking hard. Her big, dark eyes, which were as smooth and shiny as beads, gazed into Addie's.

"You know what's strange?" Sky Dance asked Addie in her high, clear voice. "I woke up this morning and had to remind myself that yesterday really happened!"

"Same here!" exclaimed Addie, and they both laughed.

Addie saw Clara holding out her palm for Shimmer Leaf to land on.

"Hello again," said Clara to Shimmer Leaf. "How was your first night as a butterfly?"

Shimmer Leaf stretched out her new wings. They were bright purple, peach, and mint green with leaf patterns. "Once I figured out how to tuck these things in for sleeping," she said, "it was great!"

The two girls and the two butterflies all giggled again, then fell silent . . . and serious.

"You called us," said Addie. "Does that mean . . ."

"Yes," replied Sky Dance. "Another New Bloom came out of her chrysalis this morning."

"It's our cousin Tiger Streak," added Shimmer Leaf.

"Was it just like with Shimmer?" asked Addie. Shimmer Leaf had woken up not knowing who she was, or that she had to grant a wish before sunset. It had taken

lots of quick thinking, plus a dash of courage, for Clara to catch the butterfly and set her free.

"We're not sure," said Sky Dance. "She flew away from the Changing Tree before we could talk to her. But she's been seen throughout the grove."

"You mean *heard* throughout the grove," corrected Shimmer Leaf.

Sky Dance sighed. "That too."

"What do you mean?" asked Clara.

"Apparently," said Sky Dance, "Tiger Streak is fluttering around making a very *un*-butterfly-like noise."

"*Bzzz*," added Shimmer Leaf.

"Like a bee?" asked Addie, frowning.

"Exactly," said Sky Dance.

"That, uh, seems like a bad sign," said Clara.

"*Exactly*," agreed Shimmer Leaf. "Will

you help us find her? We'll also need to find a human child to catch her and set her free to break the enchantment. Then Tiger Streak can grant that child a wish and earn her magic."

"We'll do whatever we can," Clara said.

"We're ready," Addie assured them.

The butterflies took flight again, and the girls followed them across the meadow. As they stepped through the entrance of Wishing Wing Grove, Sky Dance led them toward a large boulder. At first glance, it looked like someone had covered it with a thousand rainbow sprinkles. But Addie knew the boulder was crowded with dozens of Wishing Wing butterflies gathered together, each one with a dazzling combination of colors and patterns on its wings. She'd never seen anything so beautiful . . . and couldn't imagine who, or what, would want to drain these creatures of their magic.

At the top of the boulder sat Sky Dance and Shimmer Leaf's parents, Queen Rose Glow and King Flit Flash.

"Addie, Clara, my dears!" said Rose Glow. "Welcome back!"

Rose Glow's name suddenly made sense to Addie: her red, green, and silver wings sparkled in the sunlight, making the rose patterns on them light up.

"Thank you," said Addie and Clara at the same time. Sky Dance landed on Addie's shoulder, and Shimmer Leaf landed on Clara's.

"No, thank *you*," said Flit Flash. "We have our Shimmer Leaf back, and we'll be forever grateful." His wings were blue and black, with white lightning bolts on

them. They reminded Addie of a toy race car she once had.

"We did get lucky," said Addie. "Our plan worked just in the nick of time."

"Don't be so modest," chirped a cheerful voice from the boulder. "I think you had more than luck on your side."

Addie saw Madame Furia sitting next to the queen. She was the queen's green caterpillar friend, and her story was a sad one: when she was young, she'd broken a rule, and as punishment was never allowed to change into a Wishing Wing. It didn't seem to get her down, though.

"You had smarts, and you used them," continued Madame Furia. "Feel proud of that! It's another kind of magic. I know I use it." She winked at Addie, and one of her long antennae dipped forward as if she were raising an eyebrow.

BZZZ!

Something yellow, orange, and black suddenly streaked past overhead.

"That's her!" shouted Shimmer Leaf.

Another something streaked past, right behind Tiger Streak. This something was yellow and black. It also made a *bzzz* noise, but a much more natural-sounding one.

"With a bee?" asked Sky Dance.

"That bee's been chasing Tiger Streak all morning!" said the queen.

"Let's go!" Addie said, taking off after the two zigzagging insects. She could hear Clara's footsteps right behind her.

Sky Dance and Shimmer Leaf flew

straight as arrows up ahead, their wings beating fast.

Then, Addie heard a loud *thump*.

"Ow!" yelled Clara.

Addie skidded to a stop and saw Clara twenty feet behind her, facedown in a berry bramble. She ran to help her sister, grabbing her hand and pulling her up. Clara's arms and legs were covered in scratches. Tears pooled in her eyes, and she bit her lip hard. Addie knew that meant Clara was trying her best not to cry.

"Are you okay?" asked Addie, brushing some berries off her sister's shirt.

Clara just bit her lip harder and nodded.

Sky Dance and Shimmer Leaf circled back. Flit Flash and Rose Glow must have seen Clara fall, too, and flew quickly toward them. The Wishing Wing royal family landed, one by one, on a berry bush.

"We don't want anyone getting hurt," said Rose Glow. "What would you say to a quick little flight with Sky and Shimmer?"

Clara's face lit up. She knew exactly what that meant. "I would say, yes please!"

Addie laughed. "I knew you'd get your chance!"

Yesterday, the Wishing Wings had turned Addie into a butterfly for a short time. Needless to say, it had been spectacular. Clara was desperately hoping for a turn.

By now, all the butterflies from the boulder had flown over to see what was happening. They were eager to watch some very special magic that only the Wishing Wing royal family could create.

Rose Glow and Sky Dance began flying around Clara, close to each other with their wings touching, while Flit Flash and Shimmer Leaf did the same with Addie. Each pair of butterflies left a shimmering ribbon of their combined colors in their wake. Each pair flew three times around the girls.

Addie closed her eyes and could still see the colors popping behind her eyelids. When they stopped, she opened them. Everything looked different because she was smaller. Butterfly-size. She turned her head to see her wings. They were the same ones as last time: magenta and powder blue, with heart patterns.

Next to her, there was another butterfly. Her wings were deep pink and orange, like a sunset, and patterned with flames.

Ha! thought Addie. *That's my sister, all right. She's full of fire.*

"Whoa!" shouted Clara, examining her butterfly-self.

When Addie had first been turned into a butterfly, it took her a few moments to get the hang of it—she had to really think about what it would feel like to fly. But Clara sailed instantly into the air, shouting with glee.

"Come on!" called Sky Dance. "We only have a few minutes to cover as much ground as we can!"

Sky Dance fluttered away, with Shimmer Leaf behind her. Addie looked at her sister and motioned for the two of them to follow.

As they took off, the queen, king, and other butterflies soared into the air, too. Addie caught a glimpse of them, flying together in a burst of beautiful color. All that fluttering made its own warm breeze, surrounding Addie and filling her with joy.

Addie and Clara flew side by side. Clara started laughing. "This is amazing!"

It was true. Addie had never felt more free . . . or more herself. It seemed completely natural that she was a butterfly, flapping her wings, feeling the air *whoosh* by her and even through her.

But they had work to do.

"Keep your eyes peeled for Tiger Streak!" shouted Sky Dance from up ahead.

"And your ears!" added Shimmer Leaf.

The four butterflies zoomed ahead of the group and through the grove, weaving in and out of the twisty branches of the giant Changing Tree. Sky Dance led them toward the creek. Addie could see the lemon-yellow crickets gathered on the bank, and even hear their music drifting up into the air.

"Addie and Clara, fly right along the creek!" called Sky Dance. "Shimmer and I will spread out in the trees on the other side. Send us a message if you see Tiger Streak!"

Sky Dance and Shimmer Leaf headed off in another direction, while Addie and Clara flew down the middle of the creek as if it were a road. Addie scanned one side, while Clara searched the other.

Addie knew they didn't have much time as butterflies. Maybe only a few more seconds . . .

"Look!" yelled Clara. "Up ahead!"

Addie saw a fallen tree lying across the creek, and on that tree were two clusters of color. Black, yellow, orange.

"It's them!" shouted Addie. "Come on!"

Addie and Clara flapped their wings as fast as they could, aiming for an expert landing next to Tiger Streak and the bee. They were almost there.

Then, colors filled Addie's eyes again. Sparkles like on the Fourth of July.

"No!" she cried.

Splash.

Addie suddenly felt very wet and very cool, bubbles frothing around her.

She'd landed in the water. Her wings were gone, and she was big again. Her human hands and feet sank into the soft mud at the creek bottom . . . and she couldn't pull them out.

She was completely stuck.

CHAPTER THREE

"Wowie zowie!" muttered Clara, breathless. She'd plopped right into the creek, too.

"I think my hands and feet are trapped!" yelled Addie. She tugged harder, but the mud seemed to be tugging back.

Clara stood up and made her way to Addie. She wrapped her arms under her sister's, then pulled her up. Addie's hands broke free, then her feet.

"Thanks!" said Addie. "Are you okay?"

Clara nodded. Together, they made their way to the creek bank. The blue water swirled around their ankles, and Addie spied tiny pink fish just under the surface.

When they got to dry land, the girls sat on a rock and took off their sneakers, squeezing them out.

"Are Tiger Streak and the bee still there?" Addie whispered to Clara. "Can you see them?"

Clara craned her neck toward the fallen tree, then nodded. "They're still there. Lucky they didn't see us."

"Okay, good. Why don't you go talk to them? Move slowly. Let them know you're a friend."

"Just me?" asked Clara. "Shouldn't we go together?" Addie could tell her sister was both surprised and annoyed. It was a look Addie called "surpannoyed."

"Uh, well," mumbled Addie, "I was thinking that maybe the sight of two humans might scare them."

"And also, you're afraid of bees," teased Clara.

Addie felt her face flush. "That too."

"Come on, Addie. Yesterday, you let gigantic wasps chase you! That bee is nothing in comparison!"

"True . . . ," said Addie, but she wasn't quite convinced.

"Oh no!" said Clara suddenly, pointing. "They're flying away!"

Addie turned to look. Tiger Streak and the bee were in the air, but only briefly, before landing on a stone in the creek. It was a spot not far from where the girls had fallen. The two girls listened closely and could hear them talking.

"*Bzzz!*" said Tiger Streak. "I know I saw something over here! And heard something!"

"Don't worry about that right now," said the bee. "We have to get you back."

"Yes! Back to the hive! They'll notice two of their bees missing, for sure!"

Clara turned to look at Addie with wide eyes and whispered, "Tiger Streak thinks she's a bee! That's why she's making that noise!"

"It must be the enchantment," said Addie. "I'm sure that bee had something to do with it, too."

Bzzz! Bzzz!

Now Tiger Streak and the bee were

flying again, headed to the other side of the creek.

"Addie! Clara!" came Sky Dance's voice. The girls turned to see their butterfly friends zipping toward them.

"We just saw Tiger Streak," said Clara.

"And we know where she's going," added Addie. She explained that Tiger Streak must have woken up thinking she was a bee, thanks to the enchantment, and was being led back to a hive.

Sky Dance and Shimmer Leaf exchanged a confused look. Their dark eyes grew extra wide. "That doesn't make sense," said Shimmer Leaf. "The bees have always been our friends."

"All of them?" asked Addie. "Maybe these are a new group of bees."

"That's possible," said Sky Dance.

"Mother knows where all the hives are in these woods. We should go back and talk to her."

Clara jumped up. "Oh!"

"What's wrong?" asked Addie.

"I told Mom we were going for a walk, remember? She told us not to be gone long. But we totally have been! We were supposed to come back to eat!"

"It's okay," said Addie. "We'll go now." Addie hated to leave Wishing Wing Grove while there was still helping to do, but she also didn't want her mother to worry. What if she came looking for them in the woods?

Sky Dance must have read her mind. "I'll send a message as soon as I find out where all the nearby hives are," she said to Addie. "Then we can visit each one."

The butterflies led Addie and Clara out of Wishing Wing Grove, then through Silk Meadow. From there, Sky Dance and Shimmer Leaf flew off to find Rose Glow, and the girls rushed through the woods toward home. As they got closer, Addie heard Mom calling their names.

"We're here!" shouted Addie as they ran into the yard.

Mom's jaw dropped. "You were in the woods?"

"Yup," said Addie.

"The woods you're terrified of?"

"They're not terrifying anymore!" said Clara. "They're filled with—"

Addie kicked the back of Clara's leg. She didn't think Clara would blab about the butterflies, but she'd been known to spill the beans before. A reminder couldn't hurt.

"They're filled with really cool things to explore," continued Addie.

"Told you so," said Mom with a smile. "You girls ran out before breakfast. Have some lunch. You'll need energy for more exploring."

"Thanks, Mom!" said Addie.

She and Clara ran into the kitchen, grabbed a box of cereal and a carton of milk, then came back outside to sit on the steps of the deck. Addie ate straight from the cereal box with a spoon while Clara drank some milk. Then they switched.

"So," said Addie. "We were butterflies for a few minutes."

"It was incredible," sighed Clara. "Your wings were beautiful."

Clara smiled. "So were yours."

"With any luck, we'll get to do that again soon."

They were quiet for several moments, while Clara munched and Addie listened to the sounds of their neighborhood. Mom in the kitchen, running the sink faucet. An airplane flying somewhere overhead. The creak of a swing next door . . .

Next door!

Addie jumped up and ran to the tall bushes that divided their yard from Morgan's. She peeked through a bare spot in the branches and saw Morgan pushing herself on the swing.

"What are you doing?" asked Clara, coming up behind Addie.

"That's Morgan, our next-door neighbor," said Addie. "I met her this morning.

Then I was sort of . . . rude. But not on purpose! When we were talking, Sky Dance called and I had to come find you."

"She still looks pretty upset. Maybe you should go apologize."

"Tomorrow," said Addie, feeling embarrassed about what happened. She began to walk back toward the house, but Clara grabbed her arm and pulled her through the bushes toward Morgan's yard.

"Hi!" shouted Clara, waving to Morgan. "I'm Clara!"

Addie wriggled away from Clara, but

it was too late. Morgan had seen her. She stopped swinging and stared at them.

"Hi, Clara," said Morgan.

Clara walked toward Morgan. *Nooo!* thought Addie, but she had no choice but to follow her sister. Clara had always been better at meeting new people. Awkward situations didn't seem to horrify her the way they did everyone else.

"That's a cool swing set," said Clara.

"Thanks," said Morgan. "I have to stay out here until I'm ready to apologize to my brother for ruining his ball."

Clara looked confused, so Addie decided to explain. "Morgan turned a soccer ball into a face. It was really awesome."

Morgan glanced up at Addie and smiled for a second. Addie got the sense that Morgan didn't usually get compliments on her "art."

Then Addie took a deep breath and swallowed hard.

"Hey," she said to Morgan. "I want to apologize about earlier. I didn't mean to run off like that, but . . . well, I realized there was something important I had to do. I'd love to talk to you more and get the scoop on our neighborhood."

Morgan smiled again. "That would be fun," she said. "But right now I'm supposed to be feeling sorry about what I did. Maybe later?"

"Later is good," said Addie.

The girls said goodbye to one another. Addie and Clara pushed their way back through the bushes to their own yard.

"She's nice," whispered Clara to Addie. "But she also seems kind of sad."

Sad. Just like Clara had been, only a day before. When she'd really needed a wish.

"Clara!" said Addie. "Of course! Morgan is just the person we need! If we can get her to catch and release Tiger Streak, then Tiger Streak can grant her a wish! If only we knew where that buzzing butterfly was . . ."

"Well, that's easy," said Clara.

"What do you mean?" asked Addie.

Clara rolled her eyes and pointed. "Duh! Tiger Streak's right over there."

CHAPTER FOUR

Tiger Streak was hard to miss.

She was resting on a tree. Her yellow-, orange-, and black-striped wings were so bright they seemed electric. They were like little colored lights flickering on the tree's trunk.

It was also hard to miss the silly *bzzz* sound she was making.

Addie watched as the bee landed on

the tree next to Tiger Streak. She pulled Clara around to the side of the house so they wouldn't be spotted.

"If they start flying again, let's follow them," whispered Addie to Clara. "Maybe the hive is nearby."

"It is!" shouted a familiar voice. Sky Dance landed on Addie's arm.

"We must try to catch that bee before he can lead Tiger Streak there!" added Shimmer Leaf, settling onto what must be her favorite spot on Clara's shoulder. "We think their plan is to keep her until sunset, when she loses her magic."

"We found a girl who needs a wish," said Addie. "She lives right next door."

"Excellent!" said Sky Dance.

"But how do we catch a bee?" Addie asked. The thought of getting anywhere near it gave her the willies.

"Don't humans have those thingama-jigs?" asked Sky Dance. "On long sticks? We call them The Terrorizers."

"Oh!" said Addie. "You mean butterfly nets!"

"That sounds even worse!" said Sky Dance.

"We don't have any," said Clara. "Where we used to live in the city, we didn't go around catching butterflies for fun."

"Normally, I'd be relieved to hear that," said Shimmer Leaf, "if we didn't need one right now."

Sky Dance left Addie's arm and joined Shimmer Leaf on Clara's shoulder. "Shimmer?" she asked, putting her furry pink head close to her sister's. "You know . . . we can, um, make one."

Shimmer Leaf paused for a moment,

then burst out laughing. "Silly me! Of course! I keep forgetting that I can do magic!"

"It's okay," said Sky Dance, tapping a reassuring wing to Shimmer's. "You're still getting used to being a Wishing Wing." The butterfly turned to Addie and Clara. "Can you help? You know how our powers of metamorphosis work. We can change one thing into another, but it has to be . . ."

"Connected somehow," finished Addie. "I get it."

"Do we have *any* kind of net in the house?" asked Clara.

"I don't think so," replied Addie. She thought hard. *What does a net do? It catches things, but lets other things through—like air or water.* Surely they owned something that fit the bill . . .

Then a picture popped into her head.

"Be right back!" she exclaimed.

Addie ran into the house, opened a kitchen drawer, and started shuffling through. She hoped and hoped that her mother had already unpacked the item she was picturing. But it wasn't there.

"Argh!" she shouted, frustrated. Any second, Tiger Streak and the bee would start flying again, and they had to be ready to chase them. She rushed to a stack of boxes in the corner of the kitchen. She opened the box on top and started rummaging through it. Finally, at the very bottom of the box, Addie found what she was looking for.

It was a small strainer with a handle. Basically, a net! Except metal, and with very small openings. Addie sometimes used it when she helped her mom boil eggs in water. They'd empty the whole pot into the strainer. The strainer "caught" the eggs, but let the water drain through.

Once, in their old apartment, she'd seen her father trap a spider with it, then slide a piece of paper under the spider and bring it to the open windowsill, where they set it free.

Addie ran outside with the strainer and put it on the ground for Sky Dance, Shimmer Leaf, and Clara to see.

"Will this work?" asked Addie, breathless.

"Yes, indeed!" laughed Sky Dance. "I can see the connection!"

"Can I do it?" asked Shimmer Leaf. "I need the practice."

Sky Dance nodded, and Shimmer Leaf began flying in a neat circle around the strainer. She left a shimmering trail of purple, peach, and mint green as she went. Once, twice, three times she flew in that circle. A cloud of colored dust rose up from the ground.

When that dust settled, there was a butterfly net in the strainer's place. The whole thing was shiny silver that sparkled in the light.

"I was aiming to make a net that I wouldn't mind being caught in!" exclaimed Shimmer Leaf proudly. "And I do think I succeeded!"

Clara grabbed the net and waved it around. "Perfect!" she laughed.

"Look!" shouted Sky Dance, who had

flown to peek around the corner of the house. "They're on the move!"

They all followed Sky Dance. Addie saw Tiger Streak and the bee flying away from the tree. Sky Dance started chasing, and Shimmer Leaf followed close behind. Clara and Addie ran as fast as they could.

There was no time to get turned into a butterfly. *But maybe*, thought Addie, *I can tap into that butterfly spirit.* She let the memory of soaring through the air fill her head, and it felt like that memory was also powering her legs and arms and feet. Addie ran faster.

Up ahead, Addie could see Tiger Streak and the bee zigzagging toward their driveway.

They knew they were being chased now. No question about that.

The pair flew a wide loop around

Mom's car, then down the driveway and around the mailbox. Clara caught up to Sky Dance and Shimmer Leaf, but still wasn't close enough to use the net.

Back up the driveway, across the front lawn, and *boom boom boom* up the stairs to the front porch they all went. Tiger Streak flew in tiny loops, clearly terrified.

For a moment, the bee was close enough to catch.

SWISH!

Clara reached for it with the net, but missed.

Now Tiger Streak and the bee dashed across the porch, then around the side of the house toward the backyard again.

When they rounded the corner of the house to the backyard, Addie realized she'd left the door open. She watched

with horror as the bee led Tiger Streak right into the house!

Clara, Addie, and both Wishing Wings followed.

Pepper ran into the kitchen. He barked, saw all the flying things, and started chasing, too.

Great, thought Addie. *Here comes Mom any second now.*

But she heard loud music coming from upstairs. Mom was unpacking again, listening to the radio.

They all thundered through the kitchen, around the brand-new dining room table, and into the living room. When the bee led the chase toward the hallway, Addie thought, *Not upstairs! Please not upstairs!*

She let out a sigh of relief when the bee zipped right past the stairway and into the family room. Tiger Streak *bzzzed* up and down, back and forth.

"Tiger Streak, don't be frightened!" shouted Sky Dance. "It's not you we're trying to catch! It's the bee!"

"We're trying to help you!" added Shimmer Leaf.

At that, the bee slowed down. It seemed surprised.

Clara was right underneath it. Addie saw her reach up and steady the net.

Clara brought it down to the floor quickly, shouting, "I got it! I got it!"

Addie rushed to see. There was something frantically jumping around inside the net, for sure.

She felt a *whoosh* by her ear.

Addie looked up just in time to glimpse Tiger Streak flitting past her, into the kitchen and out through the open door.

CHAPTER FIVE

Addie glanced down at the very unhappy bee in the net and felt herself go into panic mode. The bee was buzzing so loudly that she was sure it was making the walls vibrate.

Pepper ran circles around the net, barking, but Clara shooed him away.

"Addie, do something!" she called. "Put the dog somewhere!"

Addie snapped herself out of it. She was happy to do anything that meant getting away from the bee. She scooped up Pepper and locked him in the downstairs bathroom. *He'll be mad,* thought Addie, *but I'd rather deal with an angry Pepper than an angry bee.*

When she came back, Clara was kneeling on the floor, her face close to the bee in the net. Sky Dance and Shimmer Leaf sat on each of Clara's shoulders.

"Did you just say something?" Clara asked the bee.

Addie moved closer, but not too close.

"Yes!" said the bee, sounding frantic and frightened. Addie could tell from his voice that he was a boy. "I said, please let me go! I'm trying to help Tiger Streak too!"

Clara glanced up at Addie, then at the

two butterflies. Each butterfly shook her wings in a kind of shrug. Clara narrowed her eyes and leaned in closer to the bee. "What exactly do you mean?"

The bee landed and let out one long, frustrated *bzzz*. Then he took a deep breath and spoke again, this time more slowly.

"When you told Tiger Streak you have to keep her safe from the bees—you were right about that. There's a whole swarm of them coming to take her to our hive!"

"Isn't that what *you* were doing?" asked Sky Dance.

"No!" cried the bee, and he threw himself against the net again.

"I don't believe him!" said Shimmer Leaf. "I bet he's trying to trick us!"

"Wait, Shimmer," said Sky Dance, dipping her antennae toward the bee.

"I think we should give him a chance to explain."

The bee sighed. "Thank you!"

"What's your name?" asked Clara.

"I'm Kirby."

"Kirby," continued Clara, "why were you with Tiger Streak in Wishing Wing Grove?"

Kirby took another deep breath. Addie drew two steps closer, to make sure she could hear what he was saying. She could see his fuzzy face and black-and-yellow-striped body. Now that he was calm, he didn't seem so scary anymore. He was actually rather . . . cute.

"This morning," Kirby began, "our queen called a hive meeting and told us that the Wishing Wings are our enemies. She didn't tell us why! She just said we were supposed to hate them from now on. So all the bees in our colony started saying bad stuff about the butterflies, and how they never liked them anyway."

"That's awful!" exclaimed Clara.

"They can't really help it," said Kirby sadly. "It's their job to just do, and think, whatever the queen tells them."

"Do you think that, too?" asked Shimmer Leaf.

Kirby puffed out his little striped chest and shook his head. "No, I don't. I've always been kind of . . . well, they call me weird. Because I tend to think for myself. It's a bad habit."

"That's a *good* habit!" said Clara.

"Not for a bee," muttered Kirby. "I get teased all the time. But still, I couldn't help it. When the queen announced that the butterflies hated us and we should hate them back, I wanted some proof. I flew to Wishing Wing Grove, and that's where I found Tiger Streak acting like a bee. I could tell there was something terribly wrong. I know a dark enchantment when I see one. I tried to explain to her that she's a butterfly, but she wouldn't listen. I kept trying, though. I kept following her."

Addie thought back to everything she'd seen in the grove. It did seem like Kirby was flying *behind* Tiger Streak. Maybe he was telling the truth.

"So you weren't leading her to a hive?"

Addie asked. She took one step closer, then stopped.

Kirby's huge, round black eyes looked Addie up and down. "No! I was trying to bring her to your queen and king."

Addie took a step back, and Kirby tilted his head at her.

"You're afraid of me, aren't you?" he asked, sounding hurt. "I can see it on your face."

"Don't mind her," said Clara. "She's afraid of anything with a stinger."

"You got hurt once," said Kirby to Addie. His voice was gentle and understanding.

"I stepped on a wasp," she replied.

Kirby nodded. "You hurt it first. By accident, of course. But that's why it hurt you back. It was afraid. We don't sting without a reason. We're not meanies like that."

"We need the bees," added Sky Dance. "They spread pollen between plants and flowers. Without them, many things wouldn't grow!"

"Don't be frightened of us," said Kirby. "The other bees think it's funny when humans are scared, but I hate being misunderstood that way."

Addie thought about that. Since yesterday, she had overcome her fear of the woods, faced down gigantic wasps, and even tried to meet a new friend. Maybe it was time to tackle this fear, too. She took one, two, then three steps, and now her feet were right at the net. She knelt down to get a good look at Kirby. Up close, he really was adorable.

"What do you think, Addie?" asked

Sky Dance, who had landed on Addie's arm. "If he's telling the truth, he could lead us to Tiger Streak."

Addie considered that, then motioned for Clara and the butterflies to follow her into the living room. This way, they could talk in private.

"I believe him," said Clara.

Sky Dance nodded. "Mama always says, assume that someone's heart is good."

Addie turned to Shimmer Leaf. "That's two votes. What about you?"

Shimmer Leaf thought for a few moments, then finally nodded. "I vote yes."

"Me too," said Addie. She led them back into the kitchen, then bent down close to Kirby.

"We're going to let you go," she told him.

"Good choice!" Kirby exclaimed. "Because I just saw the swarm outside! The queen told them to bring Tiger Streak back to our hive, but I know how to throw them off her trail."

Addie grabbed the handle of the net, took a deep breath, and lifted it up. She crossed her fingers that she wasn't going to regret this.

Kirby zoomed into the air, landed for a second on Addie's nose, and gave her what felt like a bee hug.

"Thanks!" he cried.

Addie let out a laugh. Bee hugs tickle! Then Kirby darted out the door to the deck. Addie closed the door, and they all hid behind it.

"There's the swarm!" said Clara, peeking through the window of the door.

Addie saw what appeared to be a

thick, dark, moving cloud in their back-yard. The cloud was made of flying bees! Her first thought was *ewwww*, but as she watched the bees fly so close, mirroring one another's movements, she had to admit it was also pretty cool.

Kirby raced toward the swarm and landed on the deck railing.

"Have you seen the New Bloom?" asked the swarm in unison. Their voices together sounded like a creepy chorus.

"Yes!" shouted Kirby. "She was captured by a human girl with red hair and taken inside a house!" He was doing a good job of pretending to be upset. "We can't get to her anymore!" he continued. "I'm so mad!"

"Captured?" echoed the swarm. "By a human? We have strict orders not to let that happen! 'Find the New Bloom, bring

her here. Don't let any humans catch her.'
That's what the queen said."

"I know, I was there," said Kirby, rolling his shiny black eyes. "I tried to stop her, but the human had a net."

The swarm hummed for a few moments, as if it were thinking. "We must find the girl with red hair!" it announced.

"You do that," said Kirby. "I'll stay here in case she comes back!"

The swarm changed from a round shape to a long, airplane-like shape, then flew away. When the bees were safely out of sight, Addie, Clara, and the butterflies stepped out onto the deck.

Kirby was laughing. "Ha! Did you see that! They just believed whatever I told them!"

"Why did you tell them Tiger Streak

was captured by a girl with red hair?" asked Clara.

"I wanted to keep them away from you two. *You* have dark honey hair," he said, pointing an antenna at Clara. "*You* have light honey hair," he continued, pointing the other antenna at Addie. "The swarm will leave you alone. They'll fly around the neighborhood and find no human girl. They'll go back to the hive and report their failure to the queen. They give up easily. It's really embarrassing."

"Nice trick!" said Sky Dance.

"Then we'll be free to search for Tiger Streak without them bothering us," Kirby added.

Addie smiled. Kirby *was* tricky, but in a good way. She thought of the swarm buzzing around the neighborhood, looking in vain for a girl with red hair.

A girl with red hair . . .

An image of Morgan popped into Addie's head.

Morgan . . . and her red hair!

"Oh my gosh!" shouted Addie. "We've got to go!"

CHAPTER SIX

Addie rushed toward Morgan's yard. *Yikes*, she thought. *This friendship is REALLY getting off on the wrong foot.*

"Addie!" shouted Clara, running up beside her. "What's wrong?"

"Morgan has red hair," replied Addie. "If the swarm finds her, they'll think she's the one who caught Tiger Streak!"

Clara stopped dead. "Oh. Oops."

"I'm such a dummy!" cried Kirby, who was whizzing by over their heads.

"It's okay," said Addie. "We have to find her anyway. She needs a wish. She's the one who can catch Tiger Streak and break her enchantment!"

They stepped through the bushes, and Addie scanned Morgan's yard. The swing set was empty. In the far corner of the yard, there was a garden bordered on two sides by a stone wall. The garden had definitely seen better days. A few limp flowers struggled to stand up straight, and everything else was brown and shriveled. A small wooden playhouse sat next to the garden, looking forgotten and unused.

Sky Dance and Shimmer Leaf flew into the playhouse, then reappeared.

"Nothing in there except a lot of cob-webs," said Shimmer Leaf.

"We should see if she's in the house," said Clara.

Sky Dance, Shimmer Leaf, and Kirby hid themselves behind the garden wall. Addie took a deep breath, stepped up to a bright red door at the back of the house, and knocked.

After a few moments, Mrs. Werner answered.

"Oh, hi!" she said, with a friendly smile. "Addie, right?"

"Yes. This is my sister, Clara."

Clara waved. Mrs. Werner waved back.

"Is, um, Morgan home?" asked Addie.

"She was," said Mrs. Werner. "For about two minutes, when she finally came inside and apologized to her brother about his ball." She sighed. "Then she grabbed her scooter and said she was going for a ride around the neighborhood."

Addie pictured Morgan riding her scooter alone, right into the path of the bee swarm. She felt herself go back into panic mode.

"Okay, thanks!" she called to Mrs. Werner. "Got to go!" She grabbed Clara and they started running away.

Great, thought Addie. *Now I've been rude to Morgan AND her mom.*

Clara and Addie ran down Morgan's driveway and stopped at the street. They waited for Sky Dance, Shimmer Leaf, and Kirby to catch up to them.

"We heard," said Sky Dance as she landed on Morgan's mailbox. It was painted with a big yellow sun, and Addie knew instantly it was Morgan's artwork. "Let's find her."

"I guess it's our turn to get a tour of Brook Forest," added Shimmer Leaf as she and Kirby came to rest on the mailbox as well.

"That might be a problem," said Addie. "We don't know our way around."

"We've only been to the end of our driveway," admitted Clara.

Sky Dance folded up her wings and gave Addie a look of disbelief. "You mean you haven't explored your neighborhood *at all*?" she asked.

"We just moved here!" said Addie.

"Mom kept wanting us to go for a walk, but Addie was too nervous about all the nature," said Clara. "And I was still too sad."

Sky Dance shook her head, but she was smiling. "Well, I guess now's the time."

"I'll go find Tiger Streak," said Kirby. "She trusts me. I'll meet you back at Morgan's house."

After Kirby flew off, Addie, Clara, and the butterflies set off quickly down the street. So far, Addie had only seen her new road from the car. Now that she was walking, she noticed things she hadn't before. The way the trees arched their branches over the road like a canopy. The pretty sky-blue color of the house next to Morgan's. When they reached the house after that, Addie could hear laughter and the sounds of splashing. A swimming pool!

After a few minutes, the street deadended onto another. Should they go right or left?

"I wish we had a map," said Addie. "It would be great to get a bird's-eye view of this place."

Sky Dance laughed. "You don't need a bird's-eye view, silly. You have a butterfly's eye view!"

"Oh," said Addie, laughing too. "Duh."

"Come on, Shimmer," shouted Sky Dance as the Wishing Wings soared into the air. As they went higher, they appeared smaller. From this distance, Addie couldn't even see their colors. They looked like ordinary butterflies.

Addie and Clara waited anxiously. After a minute, the butterflies fluttered back toward them.

"The street goes in a big circle!" reported Shimmer Leaf.

"We saw Morgan! She went that way!" added Sky Dance, pointing a wing to the right. "We saw the swarm, too. They went to the left. In a minute or two, they'll run smack-dab into each other."

"Come on," said Clara, turning right. Addie and the butterflies followed.

As the road started to curve, Addie could see Morgan up ahead, the bright colors of her bike helmet bobbing along.

"Morgan!" shouted Addie.

But they were too far away, and Morgan couldn't hear them.

"We won't catch up to her. She's on a scooter!"

"I have an idea," said Clara, tapping her finger on her chin. "You said the street goes in a big circle?"

"Yes," said Sky Dance.

Clara pointed at a green house on their left. "If we cut through that yard and the one behind it, we'll reach the other side of the circle more quickly. We can find Morgan before the swarm does."

"Good thinking!" whooped Shimmer Leaf.

But the thought of this made Addie cringe. "Clara, no," she said. "We're supposed to be meeting new neighbors, not barging through their property!"

"This is kind of an emergency! Besides, we'll go fast. Maybe they won't even notice."

"It's now or never," said Sky Dance.

Clara didn't wait for Addie to agree. She took off across the lawn of the green house, the butterflies flitting behind her. Addie had no choice but to follow.

They ran around the green house and into the backyard. It was filled with gnome statues. Big gnomes, small gnomes, gnome families . . . even gnome animals.

Addie almost tripped over a gnome rabbit wearing a pointy red hat.

Past that yard, there was a thicket of trees. Then, another yard. In the middle of that yard, a teenage girl lay on a blanket with her headphones on. Her eyes were closed, and she was bopping her head to music. Addie and Clara sped right past her.

Just as Clara had predicted, once they ran around that house, they found themselves back on the street . . . on the other side of the loop.

They looked left. There was the bee swarm.

They looked right. Here came Morgan on her scooter.

"Morgan!" shouted Addie, stepping directly in front of her.

Morgan skidded her scooter to a stop

and stared at them. Her long red braid peeked out of her helmet, which she'd painted with orange, yellow, and black stripes.

"Quick!" said Clara. "Tuck your hair into your helmet! Don't ask why, we'll explain later."

Morgan must have seen how panicked Addie was, so she grabbed her braid and pushed it up under the edge of the helmet.

The swarm was upon them now.

It stopped and hovered, buzzing in that creepy chorus. It moved toward Addie, then Clara, then Morgan, pausing for a moment or two above each girl. Addie held her breath.

Then the swarm continued on, down the street.

"Phew!" burst out Addie with a sigh of relief.

"Weird," said Morgan as she watched the swarm travel away from them.

There was an awkward pause. Addie glanced up to see Sky Dance and Shimmer Leaf high in the sky above.

"I love the way you painted your helmet," said Clara to Morgan, breaking the silence.

"Thanks," said Morgan. "My mom got mad at me for it, but I think this looks better than just plain white."

"We have boring helmets, too," said Addie. "Will you help us paint them?" She hoped this would be a good way to get Morgan home to her backyard.

Morgan smiled. "Yes! As long as your mom says it's okay."

"Don't worry," replied Addie. "We'll ask."

Once they all got to Morgan's backyard, Addie looked around. Where was Kirby? How long would it take him to find Tiger Streak?

Then, out of the corner of her eye, Addie saw a quick blink of orange. Then another blink of yellow. She heard an unmistakable fake-buzzing. Tiger Streak! She was fluttering near the bushes, with Kirby flying circles around her.

"Hey!" said Addie, giving Clara a nudge. "Look at that beautiful butterfly!"

Clara got the hint and spotted Tiger Streak, too. "Oh! Pretty!" she added, pointing.

Morgan glanced up, saw Tiger Streak, and said, "Wow! That's so cool!"

"Let's try to catch it," said Clara. She ran through the bushes toward their yard, then reappeared a few moments later with the net. Clara offered it to Morgan. "You go first."

Morgan shook her head. "My mom loves butterflies. She'd be mad if she knew I caught one."

"We won't hurt it," said Addie. "We'll just admire it for a minute, then let it go."

"We can take a picture of the butterfly," suggested Clara. "Then you could paint it."

Morgan paused, then smiled. "I like

that idea! I know exactly where to paint it, too."

She took the net. Addie and Clara exchanged a look. *This might work!*

Kirby left the tree and Tiger Streak followed him. They flew toward the girls, and Addie could hear Tiger Streak's buzzing get louder.

"This way!" Kirby shouted to Tiger Streak. "The queen told us we have to go this way!"

Kirby led Tiger Streak right toward Morgan. As the butterfly got closer, Morgan waved the net.

Tiger Streak was trapped inside. Morgan had caught her!

"Yes!" shouted Addie.

Just as a big, dark shadow moved over them.

CHAPTER SEVEN

It was a shadow that hummed and changed shape.

"The swarm!" shouted Clara.

When Morgan saw the bees, she jumped back and dropped the net. Tiger Streak broke free, darting away in a blur of colors.

Addie tried to see which way Tiger Streak went, but the air around her was thick with flying things, buzzing in her ear. She covered her head and started swatting at them. Clara and Morgan did the same. But it all just made the bees more furious. They grew louder, flew faster, and Addie braced herself to feel a sting . . .

"Addie!" Kirby was whispering in her ear. "Remember what I said? Bees will only hurt you if you hurt them first."

Addie nodded and shouted to the others. "Don't fight them! Let's get inside somewhere!" She saw Sky Dance and Shimmer Leaf flying to Morgan's playhouse. *This way!* Sky Dance told her in a thought message.

Addie led Morgan and Clara into the playhouse.

"Blech!" cried Clara, wiping a cobweb off her face.

"Sorry," said Morgan. "I haven't been here in a while."

Addie reached out to close the door behind them. One of its hinges was broken, so it didn't close all the way, but it was good enough. The girls huddled together on the floor. Outside, the sound of the swarm swelled and reminded Addie of raindrops, beating hard against a window.

"What do they want?" cried Morgan.

The humming paused and the swarm was silent for a moment. Then, in that single, eerie voice, it said, "The butterfly! We want the butterfly!"

Morgan gave Addie and Clara a look of alarm. "Did those bees just . . . talk to us?"

"We don't have her!" shouted Clara to the bees. "We did, but she flew away!"

"If we don't bring her the butterfly," said the bees, "she'll be very angry!"

"Tell that queen of yours she can't have Tiger Streak!" said Addie.

"And she should stop saying bad things about our friends!" added Clara.

Morgan simply sat there, looking very confused.

"Not the queen," said the swarm. "The other. The other will be angry!"

"The other?" asked Addie. "Who do you mean?"

"The one who acts like the queen of the queen!" said the swarm.

"Who's *that*?" yelled Addie. She felt as confused as Morgan must have been.

The swarm was silent for a moment, then its shadow slid away from the door.

"They left!" said Clara.

"You just had a conversation with a swarm of bees," said Morgan, shaking her head as if to wake herself up.

Sky Dance poked her little face into the crack along the doorway. "It's safe! You can come out now!"

Sky Dance disappeared. Morgan's jaw dropped open. "A talking butterfly, too?" she asked.

"We'll explain in a minute," said Addie. She pushed open the playhouse door onto the most glorious garden she'd ever seen.

The dry, brown plants were gone. They'd been replaced with dozens of flowers, nearly twinkling in the sunshine. They were purple, red, green, yellow, orange, blue, and quite a few shades in between. Two or three bees perched on each flower, happily drawing nectar.

"Not bad, right?" asked Sky Dance proudly as she hovered over the scene. "It was Kirby's idea to work some magic on the dead flowers. He knew it would distract the swarm."

Morgan stepped into the garden and looked around, her eyes wide.

"Talking bees and butterflies," she said after a few speechless moments. "My mom's depressing garden turned into *this*. Are we . . . are we talking the M-word here?"

Addie smiled. There was only one M-word, as far as she was concerned. "Could be," she said, in a way that meant *yes!*

She and Morgan were going to be good friends, Addie just knew it.

"This is great," said Clara, "but we still have to find our missing New Bloom!"

"No need for that," said a small voice from above. Something fluttered out of the air and landed on Morgan's arm.

"Tiger Streak!" exclaimed Sky Dance.

"That's me," said the butterfly. "But how did I get here? I don't even remember coming out of my chrysalis."

"You were under an enchantment," explained Shimmer Leaf. "But Morgan broke it by catching you, then setting you free."

Morgan lifted her arm so she and Tiger Streak were staring straight into each other's eyes.

"Hi," said Morgan, smiling. "We have the same style." She pointed to her orange-, yellow-, and black-painted helmet.

"Looks like I was truly meant to be your Wishing Wing!" laughed Tiger

Streak. "And now I get to grant you a wish."

"A wish," echoed Morgan.

"Choose carefully," added Tiger Streak. "You get just one."

Morgan bit her lip. "There are so many things to wish for. How does anyone choose?"

"Imagine the thing that will make you the happiest right now," suggested Addie. "That worked for me and Clara."

Morgan stared off at the garden, where Kirby and the bees were still having their own little nectar party.

"Oh!" she exclaimed, and walked past the flowers to the rock wall. Tiger Streak fluttered into the air to follow her. There were large stones and planks of wood covering one section of the wall. Morgan began removing them. Then she stepped back.

Part of the wall was painted with flowers. Morgan's work, for sure. They were as colorful as the real ones in the garden now, but smudged and messy. It was clear that Morgan kept making mistakes and trying to fix them. A few unfinished flowers had stems, but no blooms.

"I was trying to make this mural for my mom," said Morgan. "She got frustrated with the garden and gave up on it. I thought, if I could give her flowers some other way, maybe she'd finally see why I paint things that she doesn't think should be painted."

Morgan turned to Tiger Streak and took a deep breath.

"I wish . . . I wish my mom understood me and my art. Is that silly?"

"Not silly at all. Everyone wants to be understood," said Addie. She and Kirby exchanged a glance.

Tiger Streak flitted back and forth across the wall, examining the painted flowers. "I know just what to do!" she said. "But you should step back!"

Morgan went to stand next to Addie.

"Watch this," said Addie, nudging Morgan with her elbow.

Tiger Streak flew three wide circles around the wall. Glittering ribbons of orange, yellow, and black unrolled behind her. Morgan gasped at the sight of it.

When Tiger Streak was done, and the colors dissolved into the air, they could all see the result.

The wall looked like a giant painting. There were flowers, grass, a few butterflies . . . and even a bee.

"Oh my gosh," mumbled Morgan. "That's exactly what I was trying to do, but couldn't!"

"Glad I could lend a hand," said Tiger Streak. "Or rather, a wing."

"Morgan?" called a voice.

Startled, the bees flew off into the woods. The girls turned to see Mrs. Werner standing behind them. The butterflies zoomed over to the wall, hiding themselves among the painted flowers.

"What happened here?" Mrs. Werner asked, staring at the wall and garden.

"It's . . . it's a surprise for you," said Morgan.

"You did this?"

Morgan looked hurt. "The wall's ruined, isn't it? I'm sorry. I'm sorry about Calvin's ball and my helmet, and all the other things I painted that I wasn't supposed to. I just want to add some beautiful things to the world."

Mrs. Werner pulled Morgan into a hug.

"I can't believe you brought my garden back to life!" she said.

"Oh," said Morgan. "Right."

"Your mural is fantastic, and I love it. Oh, honey, all you ever had to do was talk to me about how you were feeling."

Morgan smiled big. It was the smile of a wish come true.

🦋 🦋 🦋

After Morgan and her mother went inside, Addie and Clara returned to their own yard.

They sat on the steps of the deck, cuddling with Squish. The three Wishing

Wings and Kirby whirled in circles over their heads, riding the breeze.

"Wow!" called Tiger Streak. "It feels amazing to have wings. And look at these stripes! They're as sleek as a tiger's!"

She made a tiger-like roaring noise, followed by a growl.

"No more pretending you're something you're not!" teased Sky Dance, and they all laughed.

"The next time we come to the grove, can we bring Morgan?" asked Clara.

"Oh no," said Sky Dance, growing serious. "She won't remember anything about us. Before we left, we sprinkled Forgetting Magic all over the garden. Morgan will remember that you helped her with the mural, but that's all."

"What about Tiger Streak?" asked

Addie. "Isn't she Morgan's Wishing Wing now? The way Sky Dance is connected to me, and Shimmer is connected to Clara?"

"She is, indeed," Sky Dance replied. "Morgan will feel her butterfly spirit get stronger whenever Tiger Streak is nearby. We have to use Forgetting Magic with most humans, but with you two . . . well, you're special. You were chosen to help us, and you truly have!"

"Hopefully, we'll help you some more," said Addie.

"There are still two more New Blooms under the enchantment," added Clara.

"Yes," said Sky Dance. "And now you know there's a neighborhood filled with children, just like the two of you and Morgan, who need wishes granted."

"Meeting the first new neighbor

wasn't so bad, was it?" said Clara, nudging Addie.

Addie nudged her back. It hadn't been bad at all. Actually, it had been wonderful!

Sky Dance flew up toward the roof of the house so she could peek at the sun's position in the sky. "We need to get home," she said. "Mama will be eager to hear about our adventure, and we have to introduce them to Kirby!"

Kirby flew a loop in the air. "Maybe I'll fit in better with magic butterflies than with a colony of bees who can't think for themselves," he said.

"That reminds me," said Addie. "What do you think the swarm meant about 'the queen of the queen'?"

"I'm not sure," replied Sky Dance. "I suspect the queen bee wasn't the one ordering the colony to capture Tiger Streak. She was being controlled, or influenced, by someone else."

"The same someone who's behind the enchantment!" said Addie.

"Very likely," agreed Sky Dance.

Mew, said Squish, as if he agreed, too. They all laughed.

"I think he's hungry," said Clara. "We should go inside."

"Poor Pepper!" remembered Addie. "He's still locked in the bathroom!"

"It's been a busy day," said Shimmer Leaf.

"A *magically* busy day," corrected Clara.

The sisters waved goodbye to their four flying friends, watching them disappear into the woods beyond the edge of the yard.

As she and Clara headed to the back

door, Addie looked up to
see Morgan's face in an
upstairs window of her
house. She was waving at
them. They waved back.

I have a new friend!
thought Addie. She remem-
bered what Madame Furia
said about other kinds of
magic. Friendship was
definitely one of them.

Tomorrow, maybe they'd
discover some more.

TURN THE PAGE FOR A SNEAK PEEK
AT ADDIE AND CLARA'S NEXT
MAGICAL BUTTERFLY ADVENTURE!

COMING SOON!

Sky Dance! I'm here in Wishing Wing Grove to help you. Where are you?

Addie remained quiet, her eyes shut tight. She could hear crickets in the distance. The squawk of a bird high up in a tree somewhere. The *flit-flut* of butterfly wings and the soft jingle of rushing water in the nearby creek. But nothing from Sky Dance. Addie wasn't sure this was going to work. She'd never had a magical thought connection with anything before. Was it like a telephone? Was there a way to "call" her friend?

Suddenly, her head filled not with a sound but . . . a feeling. A feeling of deep, dark sadness. It was so powerful, Addie let out a sob.

"What's wrong?" asked Clara, putting her hand on her sister's shoulder.

"She's hurting," said Addie.

"Who hurt her?" growled Shimmer Leaf. "Where is she hurting? Her wing? Her legs?"

"It's not pain in her body," said Addie, shaking her head. "It's pain in her heart."

Shimmer Leaf's antennae and wings drooped. "You mean . . . her *feelings* are hurt?"

"Yes." Addie was sure of it now.

"It must have been something Blue Rain said to her," said Clara.

Shimmer Leaf rolled her big bead-like eyes. "You've got to be kidding me. She flew away and hid because of that?"

"I can find her," said Addie, but inside she was thinking, *I think I can find her. I hope I can find her.* She closed her eyes again and listened. Now she heard something:

I am not, I am not, I am not, I am not.

Addie took a few steps, and the voice grew the tiniest bit louder in her head.

Am not! She's wrong! The thoughts from Sky Dance continued, and Addie let them guide her farther into Wishing Wing Grove. She moved past the Changing Tree, which was a huge willow with branches reaching and twisting in every direction. Then along the creek, its water clear as glass, its banks dotted with yellow crickets who shared the Grove with the butterflies and made catchy music. Sky Dance's thoughts stopped being words and changed to soft cries. Addie's feet seemed to know where they were going even if she didn't.

Eventually, Addie reached a willow tree on the edge of the creek. Its roots were thick and knotted, and underneath this tangle, there was a little cave of dirt and rocks. Addie sat on the biggest root and put her head between her legs so it hung upside down, looking into the blackness of the cave. She couldn't see anything, but Sky Dance's cries were louder than ever.

"Sky Dance? Are you in there?"

Jennifer Castle is the author of the Butterfly Wishes series and many other books for children and teens, including *Famous Friends* and *Together at Midnight*. She lives in New York's Hudson Valley with her husband, two daughters, and two striped cats, at the edge of a deep wood that is most definitely filled with magic— she just hasn't found it yet.

www.jennifercastle.com

Tracy Bishop is the illustrator of the Butterfly Wishes series. She has loved drawing magical creatures like fairies, unicorns, and dragons since she was little and is thrilled to get to draw magical butterflies. She lives in the San Francisco Bay Area with her husband, son, and a hairy dog named Harry.

www.tracybishop.com